ONCE UPON A TIME IN GHANA II

Ghana Edition

Anna Cottrell
Agbotaduah Togbi Kumassah

D1260025

Afram Publications (Ghana) Limited

copyright © 2007 Anna Cottell

The moral right of the author has been asserted

Apart from any fair dealing for the purposes of research or private study, or critism or review, as permitted under the Copyright, Designs and Patents Act 1988, this publication may only be reproduced, stored or transmitted, in any form or by any means, with prior permition in a writing of the publishers, or in the case of reprographic reproduction in accordance with the terms of licences issued by the Copyright Licensing Agency. Enquiries concerning reproduction outside those terms should be sent to the publishers.

Matador
9 De Montfort Mews
Leicester LE1 7FW, UK
Tel: (+44) 116 255 9311 / 9312
Email: books@troubador.co.uk
Web: www.troubador.co.uk/matador

ISBN: 978 1906221 58

This edition of Once Upon a Time is published by:
Afram Publications (Ghana) Limited
P.O. Box M 18
Accra, Ghana.

Tel: +233 302 412 561, +233 244 314 103
E-mail: sales@aframpubghana.com
               publishing@aframpubghana.com
Website: www.aframpubghana.com

© 2015 Anna Cottell, Agbotadua Togbi Kumassah
ISBN: 9964 70 550 6

Illustrated by: Kwabena Poku

Foreword

Both in the past and until relatively recently, storytelling has been an integral part of most traditional societies. From time immemorial good stories have been regarded as stores of knowledge and of inestimable value, record and experience. Traditional stories contain names of places, things and situations which at times no longer exist. These stories are therefore the history of the people, drawing upon the collective wisdom of a people with highly developed oral skills.

Mothers often told their children stories by the fire while cooking the evening meal to keep their minds off hunger as they waited listening with rapt attention to the stories.

Traditional stories served as a medium for relaxation and entertainment as people gathered together in the public square after a hard day's work, wishing for nothing better than to listen to a good story. These meetings constantly reinforced social cohesion and agreed values as people shared ideas before and, most significantly, after the stories.

Most eloquent public speakers were also good storytellers. The art of good storytelling requires a retentive memory with a logical, sequential and coherent presentation of situations, ideas and events. A storyteller's most effective weapon was his words as he used appreciate vocabulary, gestures and actions to bring situations and events to life, helping the listeners to use their imagination to see events in their minds' eyes.

Most traditional stories have songs which were sung at intervals throughout the story. As well as training the storyteller as a singer, the stories form a rich repertoire of the old songs composed many years ago. The songs sung during the storytelling are necessarily complementary and relevant since they reinforce the meaning of the stories.

Most traditional stories validate social attitudes towards common human characteristics such as arrogance, pride, greed, anger and laziness. They stress the consequences of such social vices as murder, adultery, robbery, lying and cheating. Retribution for wrongdoing features very strongly in many stories.

Effective storytellers were indispensable at the chief's court. Being the custodians of the oral history of the people, they were very influential in matters of traditional arbitration, especially in matters of land litigation, and succession to the stool. When new chiefs were confined prior to their outdooring, storytellers was engaged to instruct and entertain them. They were told stories of war and peace, of successful and failed chiefs, intelligent and foolish chiefs, and kind and mean chiefs with their consequent rewards and punishments.

Today, traditional storytelling no longer feature in the regular upbringing and training of our children, but rather confined to a showcase position in cultural festivals. The rich knowledge and experience embedded in the traditional stories are gradually being lost and we are intellectually, morally and emotionally poorer for the neglect. It is hoped the stories between these pages will re-enkindle the love and appreciation of them in both the old and the young.

Agbotaduah Togbi Kumassah

May 2015

Chapter 1

AYIYI AND ZOMANAGLI

Story Teller: Listen to the story
Audience: So let the story begin
Story Teller: The story falls upon Ayiyi
Audience: It falls upon Ayiyi
Story Teller: The story falls upon Zomanagli
Audience: It falls upon Zomanagli

Storyteller

Once upon a time and it was not my time and it was not your time, so once upon a time and it was not our time, there lived a very wealthy man called Zomanagli. You might think that such great riches would mean that he was happy, able to have whatever his heart desired. But, my friends, you would be wrong. Why? Draw

1

closer and I will tell you.

Zomanagli was a lonely man, having lived by himself from a tender age as one after another, all his relatives had died. Indeed, it was said that when he was a child, he was more familiar with funerals than he was with laughing and playing with friends. We also know that as a baby, Zomanagli himself had been gravely ill and had developed a hunchback. Sadness followed sadness. Unlike other young men, Zomanagli had never found a wife and still he had no wife in his later years. He grieved to think that he had no children upon whom he could lavish his affection and his wealth.

But time passed and the seasons came and the seasons went and they came and went again until it happened that a great famine fell upon the land where Zomanagli lived. Many animals perished, many crops perished, many people perished. In spite of his loneliness and his sadness, Zomanagli had remained a kind man and so he welcomed into his compound all those who were struggling to stay alive. He used his money to send to other lands where there was no famine and so he could buy food for his people. Wherever he could find healing plants he paid whatever was asked so as to bring them back to the stricken land. Everyone adored Zomanagli the saviour and, in time, the people came to regard him as their king. Much, though not all of Zomanagli's early sadness and loneliness faded.

You will understand, therefore, that it was a great and terrible shock when Zomanagli himself fell ill. All the great herbalists and medicine men of the land were consulted but no one and nothing could help. Zomanagli died and there began a period of great mourning throughout the land. Preparations were carefully made for the funeral which all would attend.

One day, in a place nearby, Ayiyi, the Spider was out hunting when he came across an old woman standing by a bundle of firewood. Seeing Ayiyi, she immediately asked,

"Oh Ayiyi, kind Ayiyi would you please help lift this firewood onto my head? I have tried to do it myself but it is far too heavy for me."

Now Ayiyi, undecided as to whether he would bother to help, nevertheless approached the old woman to take a closer look at her. As soon as he drew near, he could see that she was quietly weeping.

"Why are you crying, old woman?" asked Ayiyi,

3

4

instantly curious.

"I am crying because our friend has died."

"Who would that be?" asked Spider.

"Have you not heard of Zomanagli, the kindest and most generous person ever to have lived in our land? He was a very wealthy man but one who wanted nothing for himself. Now he has gone and, sadly, he has left no family to inherit his riches and continue his good work."

"No family, you say? That is most unusual and unfortunate. Although I never had the good fortune to meet this Zomanagli, I should like to know more about such a rare man. Tell me all that you know."

So the old woman told Ayiyi all about Zomanagli's childhood, about his hunchback and about the death of all his family when he was still young.

"As the richest man in Afatome, he could have lived a very grand life but he chose to help us instead. It is so sad that he never married and had children. He would have made a very loving husband and father."

"So why did he never marry?" asked Ayiyi.

"A hunchback is not attractive to women, especially young women who can bear children."

"No, no, of course not. Old woman, I should be most grateful if you could tell me where and when the funeral will be. I shall make every effort to be there as it is not often in this life that one gets the chance to honour such a fine person."

With his honeyed words, Spider gradually drew from the unsuspecting woman all the information he needed.

"It will be next Saturday, starting at nine in the morning. Come to Afatome and you can't miss it as everyone will be there."

"Thank you. And the burial?"

"That will follow at six in the evening, after we have all paid our full respects."

"Thank you so much, my good woman. You have been most er…. courteous. Goodbye."

"Please help me lift my load, Ayiyi."

"If I must," grumbled Spider, anxious to get away now that he had all the essential details.

So Ayiyi and the old woman went their separate ways. The scheming Spider was deep in thought. Here was an opportunity to make his fortune, an opportunity too good to be missed. His thoughts went this way and that way and that way and this way and little by little, bit by bit, a devious plan emerged from the murky depths of his spider mind.

The next morning, he awoke bright and early and set off for market where he soon found and purchased what he needed; a round earthenware pot. The day of the funeral arrived and Ayiyi attached the pot to his back, swathing both the pot and his body with length upon length of cloth before dressing himself for the funeral and setting off in good time.

As he approached Afatome, Spider started chanting:

Zomanagli is dead,
Zomanagli is dead,
But nobody sent for me.
But nobody sent for me.

My brother is dead,
My poor brother is dead,
But nobody sent for me.
But nobody sent for me.

Our mother gave birth to us,
Her lonely, forsaken children.
Two, but two of us survived.
Two, but two of us survived.

Now Zomanagli is dead,
My poor brother is dead,
But nobody sent for me.
But nobody sent for me.

Gathered together in the compound, the women heard the lament. Seeing Ayiyi's hunchback they ran to find the elders, informing them that Zomanagli's brother was nearby.

"Why did this brother never visit Zomanagli while he was alive?"

"Yes. Why should he show up now?"

"Did you know that Zomanagli had a brother?"

And so the comments continued until finally it was decided to accept the stranger's claim.

"Look at his back. He must be Zomanagli's brother."

So, according to custom, Ayiyi was given an important place at the funeral and was also asked to lead the proceedings. Puffed up with pride, he was quick to take full advantage of his position, asking to see all the properties owned by his late brother, Zomanagli. His wish was granted and soon there was a great crowd of people following, anxious to see this long-lost brother. There were those who asked him for personal favours and others who entreated him to stay in the town and continue his brother's good works.

Following Zomanagli's burial the people began feasting and drinking and Ayiyi, the ever-greedy Ayiyi, ate and drank, drank and ate to excess. Thus it was that, after many hours he made his drunken way back to the house he was staying in. He collapsed upon the bed, too drunk to think of first removing the pot from his back. During his sleep, Spider rolled from the bed onto the

9

floor, smashing the pot as he did so. Yet still he snored, on and on and on.

Shortly after daybreak, the Chief and his Elders gathered together to go through all the funeral expenses and all the donations received from those who had attended. The Chief wanted Zomanagli's brother to preside over the meeting and so he was sent for. After a while, the messenger returned saying that the newly-discovered brother appeared to be sick and unable to attend. Such news alarmed the Chief and his Elders so they set off to see for themselves.

On arriving, they made a brief tour of the compound before going up to the house itself. They knocked on the door, they called through the windows, they banged and shouted ever louder but all to no avail. After a brief consultation, they decided to force an entry. Breaking open the door they rushed into the house and began hunting high and low. Every room was scoured from top to bottom but the poor, sick Ayiyi was nowhere to be found. Their curiosity, however, was aroused by the fragments of broken pot scattered across the floor and, seeking to find and put together all the pieces, one of the searchers noticed a spindly leg protruding from a crack in the wall. One by one they pulled on the leg, gradually easing it from its hidey-hole. Out it finally came, attached to the cringing body of a spider. Not any spider but the evil impostor they had so recently hailed as the brother of their great hero, Zomanagli. These good people had been well and truly duped.

Punishment for the wicked deception he had played upon them was duly decided upon and Ayiyi, desperate to escape the beatings, rushed to hide in a dark and remote corner of the room where he prayed he would not be discovered. And so it was and so it is from that day to this that Spider skulks nervously in obscure nooks and crannies, ready to scuttle away at the first approach you or I may make.

Story Teller:	*This is the story an old lady told me on my way here to meet you.*
Audience:	*Is that so? Then long may your tongue be oiled.*
Story Teller:	*And long may your ears be greased.*

Storytelling village: Klikor

Chapter 2

THE CHIEF AND NYANUWUFIA

Storyteller: Listen to the story
Audience: So let the story begin
Storyteller: The story falls upon the Chief
Audience: It falls upon the Chief
Storyteller: The story falls upon Nyanuwufia
Audience: It falls upon Nyanuwufia

Story Teller

Once upon a time and it was not my time and it was not your time, there was a village where it was customary for the Chief himself to choose the name for all the babies born to women who lived in his village. One day, a woman called Azazu gave birth to a beautiful baby boy and she came to the Chief to ask for a name for him. So the Chief took the baby and spent time gazing at him and pondering a suitable name for such a fine infant. However, before the Chief spoke, the baby opened his mouth and said,

"When I was in my mother's womb, I heard you naming all the newborn babies but I have already chosen my name. It is Nyanuwufia, meaning, as I think you know well, 'I am cleverer than the Chief'."

Both the Chief and Azazu were speechless. How could this be? Never before had they heard a newborn baby speak. Never before had anyone chosen a name, and such a name 'I am cleverer than the Chief.'

Shocked, of course; angry, most definitely; BUT also intrigued by this baby, the Chief kept a very close eye on his development and so when the boy reached his eighteenth birthday, he summoned him to the palace.

"What is your name?" he asked.

"My name is Nyanuwufia,"

"Come here and take these grains of maize and go and plant them on rocky ground. When the maize is fully grown, harvest it and bring it to me!" ordered the Chief.

So, protecting himself from the curiosity and

mockery of others, Nyanuwufia disguised himself and went to make the rocky ground ready for sowing. Suddenly, the Chief appeared.

"What are you doing, boy?" asked the Chief.

"I'm preparing this rocky ground so that I can sow the maize seeds I have here."

"How can you be so stupid? You can't possibly plant them on this rocky ground."

"I know that and you know that full well but it was you who told me to plant them here," replied Nyanuwufia, handing the grain back to the Chief.

Time passed as the hours turned into days and the days turned into weeks and then it so happened that one day, the Chief sent for the boy again.

"What is your name, boy?"

"My name is Nyanuwufia."

"Take this lamb, rear it and when it is fully grown into a ram, have it mated so that it will give birth to a new lamb."

The boy said nothing but took the lamb home where he tied it to a stake in the compound. Picking up an axe, he went to the Chief's compound and began cutting down a mango tree which provided shade. Naturally enough, the Chief came out to see what was going on.

14

"What do you think you are doing, impudent boy?"

"My father is in the last stages of labour and I must have wood to heat water."

"How can a man possibly be in labour? A man will never give birth to a child."

"I know that and you know that full well but it was you who told me to take an infant ram and rear it until it could give birth to a lamb."

"Fetch me the ram!" commanded the Chief.

No sooner had Nyanuwufia appeared with the ram, than the Chief found another test for him.

"Fetch me a live hog!"

So once again, the boy set off to do as he was told. Taking a long pole and a rope, he walked in the forest for many hours before he saw a hog feeding. He was careful to approach it cautiously and keep a respectful distance as he said,

"The Chief of my village thinks he knows everything and is determined to prove his superiority in all things. He has therefore ordered me to take him a live hog as he is convinced that it is impossible to tie one to a pole, strong and fierce as you all are. I would be most grateful if you would help me show him just how wrong he is."

Fortunately for Nyanuwufia, the hog took a liking to him and obligingly lay down, wrapped his four legs around the pole while he was tied on, ready to be transported back to the Chief. It was a long, exhausting journey but eventually the two of them arrived at the palace. The Chief was truly amazed but still unwilling to admit that Nyanuwufia merited his name, 'I am cleverer than the Chief.

"Fetch me a live python!" came the command and so, taking a pole and a rope once again, Nyanuwufia travelled through the forest until he came to a clearing where he saw a python coiled up in the sun, sleeping off the effects of a heavy meal. As soon as the python saw the boy, he prepared to strike him but Nyanuwufia broke in quickly, saying,

"Can you see this pole? The Chief of my village asserts that it is longer than you, the mighty python. I am offering you the chance to prove not only your superior length and strength but also that the Chief is wrong."

Nyanuwufia's clever words did the trick as the python stretched his body along the pole while he was tied on and Nyanuwufia hoisted the pole onto his shoulders and carried him back to the Chief. The Elders fled in terror as soon as they saw the snake but the Chief held his ground and redoubled his efforts to find a task which would defeat Nyanuwufia.

"Fetch me Death!"

This time, Nyanuwufia took a large wicker basket and some okra which he crushed to a sticky pulp and spread all over the inside of the basket. As he went he sang:

Death, Azagidi, my Chief has spoken.
Death, Azagidi, come home with me.
Death, Azagidi, my Chief has spoken.
Death, Azagidi, come home with me.

All of a sudden, the boy saw Death reclining in an armchair in front of his own house in the forest. Hair covered his body from head to toe and he was smoking a pipe. A strange and unexpected image indeed!

"What do you want, child?" asked Death. Concealing his anxiety, Nyanuwufia replied in his usual confident voice,

"Look at this wicker basket. My Chief claims that you will never allow yourself to appear, carried in a basket such as this. He also claims to understand all your thinking and to know all your ways so I thought you might like the opportunity to prove him wrong, once and for all time."

"I am very happy to oblige. Your Chief sounds particularly pompous, a characteristic most unsuited to the role of Chief."

So Death climbed into the basket where Nyanuwufia tied him in securely and carried him home, singing as he went,

Death, Azagidi, my Chief has spoken.
Death, Azagidi, come home with me.
Death, Azagidi, my Chief has spoken.
Death, Azagidi, come home with me.

"I have brought you Death, my Chief," announced

Nyanuwufia as he entered the palace compound. Placing the basket on the ground before the Chief, he tipped it up and Death slid out, gliding across the okra pulp with silent ease and then attacking the Chief. Death was quick to overpower this, his first victim and then, with a taste for more, he sought out and killed all the Elders before returning to his own village.

Nyanuwufia was duly enstooled as Chief of the village but from that day forward, Death is no longer content to pass all his time reclining in an armchair in front of his house. For us and for all there is no knowing when he will visit or whom he will visit or indeed how many he will visit. So it was that from that day to this and for as far as we can see into the future, Death, the grim Reaper has dominion over all living things.

Storyteller:	An old lady told me this story on my way here to meet you.
Audience:	Is that so? Then long may your tongue be oiled.
Storyteller:	And long may your ears be greased.

Storytelling village: Dzelukope

Chapter 3

THE TORTOISE AND THE LIZARD

Story Teller: Listen to the story
Audience: So let the story begin
Story Teller: The story falls upon the Tortoise
Audience: It falls upon the Tortoise
Story Teller: The story falls upon the Lizard
Audience: It falls upon the Lizard

Story Teller

Once upon a time, in a far-off place, there was a very big, very dense tropical forest with tall, tall trees stretching ever upwards towards the light. A glorious and exuberant abundance of life pulsated all around as plants, birds, insects and all manner of animals lived side by side as they have always done, sometimes in harmony and sometimes in discord. Now let us make our way to one small village tucked away, deep in the forest.

As we have said, our story falls upon the Tortoise and the Lizard and we will find them close to their village, bathed in a brilliant shaft of sunlight penetrating the dense forest canopy. Tortoise and Lizard were old friends, having known each other since childhood and, as good friends do, they enjoyed the time they spent together. However, one significant fact came between them. Lizard was very poor and had to live a humble life while Tortoise enjoyed great wealth and all the pleasures his money could buy.

Yet there was also another important difference between these two; poor Lizard was exceptionally handsome whereas rich Tortoise was exceptionally ugly. Jealousy raged inside Tortoise as he watched the admiring glances his friend enjoyed and so it happened that he fell to scheming against his old friend. He resolved to use his wealth to seduce the most beautiful creature in the village. Understand, my friends, that this beautiful gecko, for gecko she was, happened to be Lizard's wife.

First, Tortoise showered both Lizard and his wife with gifts and then he began to visit them regularly until it was quite normal for him to be seen entering and leaving Lizard's compound. One day he arrived when Lizard's wife was alone in the house. Seizing the opportunity he had been waiting for, Tortoise set about seducing her.

"You must know that you are all I desire in this world. Why do you allow yourself to live in drudgery when I, Tortoise can offer you all that your beauty and youth deserve; fine clothes, exquisite jewellery and a beautiful house furnished with the best that money can buy?"

What young girl could possibly resist such an offer? Surely only a fool would choose poverty and misery. And so it was that Tortoise and Gecko left Lizard's house together.

When Lizard arrived home and realised what had happened he was very angry but, being poor, he had nothing to offer his wife who was indeed enjoying a life of luxury with Tortoise. So Lizard withdrew from the pitying gaze of the other villagers and lived in solitude. Only he knew that he was quietly watching and waiting,

23

feeling sure that one day he would be able to take his revenge.

Time passed and time passed far away in the deep forest as the hours turned into days, and the days turned into weeks, and the weeks turned into months and the months turned into years until one day Lizard heard that the mother of his ex-wife had died. Great was his astonishment when the following morning he was woken by a loud knock on his door and upon opening it, he saw his former friend, Tortoise.

"Good morning, Lizard. I hope I find you in good health."

"Good morning, Tortoise. What a pleasant surprise. Yes, I am indeed in the best of health, thank you. You are welcome. Please come in."

Assuming that after all this time Lizard had forgiven him for taking his wife, Tortoise gave a full account of his mother-in-law's death and of the funeral plans and finished by asking Lizard to accompany him to the ceremony. As he listened, a plan began to take shape in Lizard's mind and so he replied,

"Well, this is upsetting news, my friend. Of course I should deem it a great honour to join you at the funeral."

24

"Thank you very much, Lizard. May I ask you to wear the beautiful red velvet cloak I know you have as it makes you look so elegant."

"I shall fetch it from my wardrobe now and make sure it is freshly pressed," said   Lizard, knowing

all the while that it was because of his own ugliness that Tortoise wanted the handsome Lizard to be seen with him, resplendent in the wonderful gown he had inherited from his father and which he only wore to important funerals.

As dawn broke on the day of the funeral, Tortoise and Lizard set off for the village where mother-in-law had lived and, on the way, they came to a stream which they were obliged to cross.

"You know I can't swim," said Lizard. "Surely you had thought of this when choosing the route. I will give you a donation for the funeral and you must give it in on my behalf as I shall now return home."

"I'm really sorry, Lizard, I had not given the stream a thought. I don't want you to go back now. Listen, I have an idea."

Several ideas were discussed before Lizard hit upon his master plan.

"Open your nostrils wide and then I can climb into your nose and stay safe and dry while you swim across the water," suggested Lizard.

So this they did but upon reaching the far bank,

Lizard groaned and said,

"I'm not feeling very well, having been so close to the water. I think I'll stay here a while longer. You just keep walking, Tortoise."

Tortoise's eventual arrival in the village was met with a warm welcome.

"Tell them that you have a friend with you. We shall need food for two," instructed Lizard.

Accordingly, after the burial, Tortoise's in-laws provided generous portions of food and drink.

"Come out and share this feast with me!" hissed Tortoise to Lizard.

"No, I'm very snug here now. You feed me, my friend."

"Certainly not! I draw the line at that" replied Tortoise, feeling increasingly cross, not to say uncomfortable with the constant pressure in his nostril.

Resolute, Lizard started to scratch, scritch, scratch inside first one nostril and then creeping into the other he continued his scratching, scritching, scratching until Tortoise cried out in pain.

"Stop! For pity's sake, stop!"

"Not until you feed me."

Not a morsel entered Tortoise's hungry mouth as Lizard gorged himself on everything that came near him. Whenever Tortoise thought that he himself would snatch a little something to ease his hunger, he had only to lower his head near the dish and, quick as a flash, out darted Lizard's tongue and then down, down went the food, down into Lizard's stomach.

And so the evening became night, and only then did Tortoise's wife come to lead her husband to the house where he was to sleep. Bidding him a good night's rest she returned to her family.

Only once Tortoise, weary and faint from hunger, had crawled into bed and fallen fast asleep, did Lizard come out into the bedroom. The anger and hurt that he had suffered at the loss of his wife to the treacherous Tortoise finally unleashed itself. He ran up and down the walls, over the bed and across the floor, emptying the contents of his stomach as he went, before settling himself back in Tortoise's nostril.

In the morning, Tortoise's wife came to the bedroom to see her husband. Such was the dreadful stench that she came no further than the door which she opened and quickly closed as she caught sight of her husband, covered in stains, excrement and vomit. In desperation, Tortoise began calling to her:

> "Do not leave me, my wife.
> Come and help me, my wife.
> My stomach keeps running,
> My gut keeps running.
> Do not leave me, my wife.
> Come and help me, my wife."

In spite of his repeated cries, no help came and so Tortoise, deeply ashamed to be in such a state, decided to return home. Having safely crossed the river, Lizard knew that it was time to leave his hidey-hole. Gleefully he slid out onto the ground and faced Tortoise.

"Well my friend, what did you think of mother-in-law's funeral? Did the arrangements all go according to plan? Delicious food, wasn't it?"

Tortoise did not reply; not a grunt, not a groan.

"If I caused you pain, if I caused you shame, then think of the pain and the shame you caused me when you took my wife away from me," said Lizard, referring for the first time to the great wrong that Tortoise had done him many years before.

Unable to stay and face his childhood friend, Tortoise turned and set out on another journey, leaving for ever the village of his birth. As he went he sang very softly, fearful of attracting attention to himself:

> *Awudi went to war*
> *And overcame Sanze.*
> *Awudi went to war*
> *And overcame Sanze.*
> *He went to Adza and he went to Ayo*
> *He went to Adza and he went to Ayo.*
> *But finally, this great captain*
> *Returned, defeated.*
> *But finally, this great captain*
> *Returned, defeated.*

From that day forth, Tortoise shunned all company as he took himself off, deeper and deeper into the forest. Where will you find him now? Why, hidden amongst the trees and by the streams.

So remember this, my friends: never look for kindness in the friend you have betrayed. If you do, you will discover that in love as in war, there is and can only ever be the victor and the victim, the conqueror and the conquered.

> **Story Teller:** *This is the story an old lady told me on my way here to meet you.*
>
> **Audience:** *Is that so? Then long may your tongue be oiled.*
>
> **Story Teller:** *And long may your ears be greased.*

Storytelling village: *Klikor*

Chapter 4

THE SNAIL AND THE MONKEY

Storyteller: Listen to the story
Audience; So let the story begin
Storyteller: The story falls upon the Snail
Audience: It falls upon the Snail
Storyteller: The story falls upon the Monkey
Audience: It falls upon the Monkey

Storyteller

Now it so happened that once upon a time there was a snail and a monkey – an oozing, glooping, 'my thoughts to myself' sort of a snail and a scattering, chattering, leaping sort of a monkey and these two were great friends. Odd that, a monkey and a snail. Still, it was so, deep in the forest far away across the sea in Africa.

One day, however, Monkey was feeling rather grumpy and so he said to Snail, "Just because I can climb trees much better than you, I really don't see why I should always be the one who, day in day out, breakfast, dinner, tea, morning, noon and night goes out hunting for food. Wh…….."

Before he could say another word, Snail cut in indignantly,

"Hey! Who says you can climb trees better than I can? Where's the proof?"

"So you want proof, do you? In that case, you'd better do something about it. I can't recall a single time when you have gone out doing anything very much and certainly not hunting for our dinner, climbing to find the tenderest, juiciest leaves high up in the tree

"I'll go now then and not only will I climb but I'll get to the very top of the trees before you," retorted Snail, piqued by his friend's remarks.

"No, wait! That's just silly. I want a proper fight. Look at you, you're all flab and oozy bits. There's not a muscle to be seen, not from where I'm standing

33

anyway. Why don't I carry on for a week while you do some intensive training? Whatever you say, you cannot dispute that you're out of shape right now so if you're really serious about proving that you can climb right to the top of the trees better than I can, you should follow a fitness programme straight away."

We move on a week until the competition day dawned and the two friends stood side by side in the forest where they had a multitude of trees to choose from; tall trees, short trees, fat trees, thin trees, old trees and young trees.

"Who goes first?" asked Monkey.

"You can," replied Snail, suddenly feeling a little anxious. After all, one week's training is not much when you are facing a big challenge.

Scarcely had Snail uttered the words before Monkey was off, scampering up the trunk of the nearest tree and then jumping and leaping from branch to branch, from tree to tree. Such agility and confidence are a joy to see unless, like Snail, you are about to compete in the same event.

"Come on, Snail! How long do I have to wait for you to start? Are you coming this year or next? Get

going now and perhaps your slimy body will make it to the second branch by next year!"

Spurred into action by Monkey's taunts, Snail started up the trunk of the tallest tree and then, leaf by leaf, twig by twig, branch by branch he slithered and oozed his way ever upwards. Meanwhile, Monkey was out of sight but could be heard whooping and calling to all those he thought might catch sight of him as he swung his way through the forest. So happy was he that he had more or less forgotten about Snail and the competition.

"So where are you, Monkey?" called Snail.

Monkey came leaping back, keen to tease his tiny friend.

"So where are you? Have you left the ground yet?"

Monkey, climb through the trees
Monkey, climb through the trees
Monkey, look up. Monkey, look up.
Monkey, leap through the trees
Monkey, leap through the trees
Monkey, look up. Monkey, look up.
Monkey, swing through the trees

Monkey, swing through the trees.
Monkey, look up. Monkey, look up.
Monkey, whoop through the trees
Monkey, whoop through the trees
Monkey, look up. Monkey, look up.
Monkey, climb through the trees
Monkey, leap through the trees
Monkey, swing through the trees
Monkey, whoop through the trees
Monkey, look up, Monkey look up,
Monkey look up, Monkey look u..................p!

Monkey looked up and he looked up and he looked up and he saw nothing. There was simply no sign of Snail. Or was there? As he looked, he suddenly noticed a shiny trail leading up from the bottom of the trunk, up over the leaves, up the trunk, up over a twig, up the trunk, up over a branch again and yet again, finally ending at the very summit of the tree where, just a speck in the distance, Monkey saw Snail balancing on the flimsiest leaf he had ever seen.

"What are you waiting for? The view from up here is simply superb, isn't it? As I turn I can see elephants bathing, lions roaming, giraffes eating, cattle grazing. In

the distance there are huts and houses, people working, people living together. Tell me, my friend, which view do you like best? Do you prefer to face north, south, east or west?" shouted Snail triumphantly.

All of a sudden, Monkey's voice became very subdued so that Snail could only just make out his words.

"I don't know. I have never seen what you can see."

"That's really sad. You are missing the very best part of climbing. Come on up now. I'll wait for you," encouraged Snail.

"I can't. There is no leaf, however broad, however long, however strong which will support me."

Feeling thoroughly beaten and ashamed, Monkey slunk off into another part of the forest, far away from all the places he had known and enjoyed with Snail.

So it was and so it is from that day to this that the monkey keeps to his own kind, avoiding all other inhabitants of the forest who might just remember his shameful defeat by the humble snail.

Storyteller: This is the story an old lady told me on my way here to meet you.

Audience:	Is that so? Then long may your ears be greased.
Storyteller:	And long may your tongue be oiled.

Storytelling village: Dzelukope

Chapter 5

THE HIPPOPOTAMUS AND THE ELEPHANT

Story Teller: Listen to my story
Audience: So let the story begin
Story teller: The story falls upon the Hippopotamus
Audience: It falls upon the Hippopotamus
Story Teller: The story falls upon the Elephant
Audience: It falls upon the Elephant

Story Teller

Once upon a time it so happened that there was a Hippopotamus and an Elephant living in the same ancient forest, in the same ancient land which had been called home by all manner of bird and beast since a time beyond counting.

41

Although they came from different families, the Hippo and the Elephant were true friends, having known one another for as long as they or anyone else could remember. In the manner of all good friends, they played together, they joked together, they teased one another and they supported one another. But in the way of all creatures, there were days when they engaged in bouts of rivalry, in trials of strength and it is upon such a day as this that we join our two friends, the Hippopotamus and the Elephant.

"Have you any idea of just how strong I am?" Hippo asked Elephant, proudly flexing his muscles.

"I've never noticed any more muscles on you than on anyone else. In fact, I'd go so far as to say that you look overweight rather than strong," replied Elephant, beginning to relish the argument.

"Are you calling me obese?"

"Seeing as you mention it, I think you should go and have your weight checked."

"I'll ignore your rudeness and get back to my original question. Do you understand just how strong I am?" asked Hippo, struggling to control his anger.

"So it's a tug of war you want then," replied Elephant

very confidently.

"Good idea. The first one to pull the other into the river is the winner," asserted Hippo, equally if not more confident.

"Fine! Let's go then."

They set off at a good pace, eager to show their prowess. Bragging to all they passed on the way, each gathered a band of supporters willing to cheer their chosen hero and boo his opponent. Half an hour's steady trot brought them all to the river bank where they prepared for the great trial of strength. Hippo attempted a few unconvincing press-ups while Elephant chose head and leg stretching, again rather unconvincingly.

Urged on by their impatient and rowdy supporters, the two protagonists squared up to one another, took a firm grip on the rope and started to pull with all their might.

First Elephant was pulled into the water and then Hippo was dragged in and so it continued, backwards and forwards. The cheers and boos got louder and louder as more and more creatures joined the crowd, eager to enjoy the spectacle. The contest drew to a climax as Elephant, up to his chest in water but not

down, summoned up a last almighty display of strength and, still pulling on the rope, heaved himself back onto the land where he did a quick half turn and catapulted himself backwards into the river. Back, back, back, he went, dragging the rope and his rival after him at such a speed that poor Hippo, taken completely off his guard, lost his footing and disappeared under the water. His fickle supporters quickly deserted him and joined in with the cheering for the victorious Elephant who began his triumphal song:

> *It's me the Elephant, it's me the Elephant.*
> *You'll never pull me in, you'll never pull me in.*

> *It's me the Elephant, it's me the Elephant.*
> *You'll never ever see me living in the water.*

> *It's me the Elephant, it's me the Elephant.*
> *You're not as strong as me, you're not as strong as me.*

> *It's me the Elephant, it's me the Elephant.*
> *You'll never pull me in, you'll never pull me in.*

Meanwhile, poor Hippo, the once-proud Hippo, eventually regained his footing but not his pride as, hoping to make his escape unnoticed, he tried to leave the water further downstream, away from the crowd.

Imagine, my friends, his horror when he discovered that the rope had become wound round his body and had snapped under his own weight, under the very weight he had refused to recognise.

Full of shame, Hippo remained concealed in the river and that is where you will probably find him still, safer and more at ease in the water than on dry land.

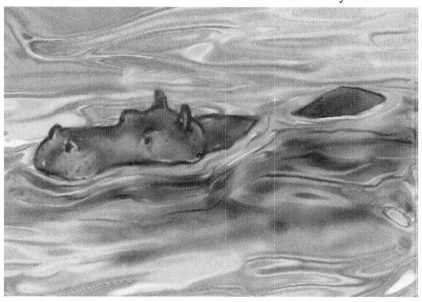

As for the rest of the rope, it remained with Elephant who decided to cut it in two and wear both pieces as a badge of honour. Where? Well, where do you think the Elephant's two magnificent tusks come from?

Story Teller: This is the story an old lady told me on my way here to meet you.

Audience: Is that so? Then long may your tongue be oiled.

Story Teller: And long may your ears be greased.

Storytelling village: Dzelukope

Chapter 6

THE HAWK AND THE TORTOISE

Storyteller: Listen to the story
Audience: So let the story begin
Storyteller: The story falls upon the Hawk
Audience: It falls upon the Hawk
Storyteller: The story falls upon the Tortoise
Audience; It falls upon the Tortoise

Storyteller

Now it so happened that there was once a Hawk and a Tortoise who were very close friends, having known each other all their lives. One day the two were together, chatting about this and that when the news arrived that Hawk's mother-in-law had died. As soon as Hawk heard this he asked Tortoise to accompany him to the funeral, explaining that he felt that in view of their lifelong friendship, they should share an event as significant as the funeral of a close relative.

"Of course," agreed Tortoise. "I shall obviously need much more travelling time than you so I will set off today. It would be a great help if you would at least take my luggage with you."

"I shall certainly do that," agreed Hawk. "Just leave it outside your house and I'll fetch it when I am ready to go myself, first thing tomorrow morning. Leave a bit of room for my robes and then I only need to carry one case. See you there."

"Thanks. Safe journey!" called Tortoise as he set off for home.

Arriving at his house, Tortoise ate a meal and fetched his suit-case which he placed outside his house. Thereupon he climbed inside, hid himself beneath his funeral robes, pulled the lid down and waited.

The following morning, Hawk arrived, lay his robe on top of Tortoise's, picked up the case in his beak and flew to the wedding.

Upon his arrival, he added the luggage to that of the other guests in a room put aside for them all and went off in search of Tortoise.

As soon as he was alone, Tortoise pushed up the lid of the suitcase and crawled out. Donning his elegant robe, he joined the funeral guests where he was soon spotted by his friend, Hawk.

"Where have you sprung from? I've been looking everywhere for you. I thought you must have got lost."

"I did take a couple of wrong turnings and that delayed me but I suppose I've been here about twenty minutes now. Just time to find my suitcase and get properly dressed," answered Tortoise.

"Well, your finery is putting me to shame so now I'll go and get myself sorted. I'm happy to know you've finally made it here anyway."

Everyone was pleased to see Tortoise and so he felt that his little trick was justified. Hawk was especially happy to have his friend at the funeral and it wasn't long before Tortoise began thinking about how he would get home as Hawk was not going back for a few days, although he was happy to take the suitcase once again. Fortunately for Tortoise, he fell into conversation with Hawk's brother who was collecting together the piles of rubbish that had been dropped

"So what is going to happen to all this rubbish?" Tortoise asked.

"There's a new tip about to open. Come to think of it, you have probably heard of it as it's only a mile or so from you."

52

"I didn't realise that it had already opened," replied Tortoise.

"Well, strictly speaking, it doesn't open until tomorrow but we have managed to get permission to use it today. As soon as everyone's gone, I shall take this rubbish over there myself. I think my cousin will give me a hand but I thought I'd start gathering it together," explained Hawk's brother.

At that very moment, the bird was called away and so Tortoise cunningly hid himself among the rubbish. Just as Hawk's brother had said, once all the guests had departed, he and his cousin picked up the refuse and flew with it to the new tip. All that Tortoise had to endure was a brief spell of travel sickness and a bumpy landing but seeing that he was nearly home, he accepted all that as a necessary but temporary inconvenience.

A few days later, Hawk called round to see how Tortoise was feeling.

"Thank you so much for all the effort you made to be at the funeral with me. I've been a little bothered as you seemed to disappear towards the end and nobody else knew where you were either," said Hawk.

"There are times when life needs serious

management, my friend," Tortoise replied enigmatically as he ambled off in search of a few leaves for lunch.

Storyteller:	This is the story an old lady told me on my way here to meet you.
Audience:	Is that so? Then long may your tongue be oiled.
Storyteller:	And long may your ears be greased.

Storytelling village: Have

Chapter 7

THE ELEPHANT AND THE TORTOISE

Story Teller: Listen to the Story
Audience: So let the story begin
Story Teller: The story falls upon the Elephant
Audience: It falls upon the Elephant
Story teller: The story falls upon the Tortoise
Audience: It falls upon the Tortoise

Story Teller

Once upon a time, a time beyond counting, deep, deep in a large forest there lived a big Elephant while at the edge of the forest there lived a tiny Tortoise. One day the Tortoise was out looking for food when he met the Elephant. They soon became firm friends; the Elephant liked the Tortoise because he was so small and the Tortoise admired the massive size of the Elephant.

Some time later, it happened that the Tortoise decided to pay Elephant a call. Upon his arrival at his friend's compound, Tortoise was greeted by Elephant's children who were playing happily together.

"Hello children. I am a friend of your father. Is he in?" asked Tortoise.

"Yes, he's having a nap but we'll go and wake him if you like," replied the children.

"Yes please."

Whereupon the children ran into the house, eager to wake Elephant and tell him of his friend's arrival. Such was their excitement that they almost forgot to pick up the huge hammers they needed to rouse their father from his deep slumbers. It took several minutes of heavy hammering upon his back before Elephant stirred, rubbed both eyes and rather grumpily asked,

"What's all this noise about then? Can't I enjoy forty winks without being disturbed by you?"

"Wake up, Dad! Your friend Tortoise is here."

"What, here in our compound?"

"Yes, yes. Come and see him!"

So Elephant heaved himself out of bed just as quickly as he could and went to greet his tiny friend. They chatted happily together while the children went back to their game.

"You will be hungry and thirsty after your journey," said Elephant. "You must eat with us before setting off again."

So saying, Elephant set to, preparing a delicious meal for Tortoise and he also offered him palm wine to drink in honour of their friendship. Feeling very contented, Tortoise bade his friend goodbye and set off for home, but not before inviting Elephant for a return visit.

On the way home, Tortoise fell to thinking about being woken with a hammer.

"How exciting that must be! I'm sure none of my tortoise family or friends have been woken like that," said Tortoise to his imaginary audience.

Thereupon, Tortoise started planning Elephant's return visit. First he went to the blacksmith where he ordered two large hammers which he was able to collect the following day. All that remained was to explain to his children exactly what they had to do and when.

The appointed day arrived and Elephant set out for Tortoise's house. As he approached, Tortoise's children who had been waiting very impatiently just a short distance from their compound, rushed back home as fast as their little tortoise legs would carry them to tell their father to prepare himself for the arrival. Then they greeted Elephant as he reached the compound.

"Good morning, Elephant. Welcome to our home!"

"Thank you, my children. How are you?"

"We are fine, thank you. And you, Elephant, are you well?"

"Yes, I am fine also. Is your father here?"

"Oh yes, Elephant. We'll go and fetch him for you."

In a trice, they rushed indoors, picked up the hammers and, recalling exactly what their father had told them, they began hitting his shell. Bang! Bang! Bang! Tortoise was soon groaning aloud in pain but still the children hammered as hard as they could until his shell broke into pieces of all shapes and sizes. The dreadful groans brought Elephant into the room where he was horrified to see the state Tortoise was in.

"Stop, children, stop! Your father will die if you continue hitting him like that. Look at his shell. A broken shell is of no use to him."

Immediately, Tortoise's children stopped their hammering. Elephant slowly crossed the room, singing softly to his poor friend as he approached him:

> "Tortoise, you dreamed of being woken with a hammer
> But the hammer will break your shell.

Your shell is not my skin.
The hammer will break your shell.
Tortoise, you dreamed of being woken with a hammer
But the hammer will break your shell."

Elephant bent down and carefully lifted his tiny friend, collecting all the fragments of shell. Then he set off straight away for the medicine man who was able to sew all the pieces together again. In time, the wounds

60

healed as they should, but the stitches left many scars which you may see to this day. So, my friends, now you know why the tortoise has a patched shell which he must wear for evermore.

Story teller: This is the story an old lady told me on my way here to meet you.

Audience: Is that so? Then long may your tongue be oiled.

Story Teller: And long may your ears be greased.

Storytelling village: Klikor

Chapter 8

THE CHILDREN AND THE HYENA

Storyteller: Listen to my story
Audience: So let the story begin
Storyteller: The story falls upon the Children
Audience: It falls upon the Children
Storyteller: The story falls upon the Hyena
Audience: It falls upon the Hyena

Storyteller

Once upon a time, not here, not there but somewhere in a distant African past, there lived a hunter who, in order to supplement his income, was also a farmer, having been fortunate enough to inherit some land from his father. As he could not spare much time to work on the farm, the hunter always took his Children to help every time he visited his land.

It therefore seemed very strange when one day he decided to visit the farm taking only his wife. The Children complained loudly, after the manner of children who feel they are being denied a treat. However, their father remained steadfast and set off for the farm, instructing the Children not to squabble and fight while they were left alone for a few hours. When their parents had not returned by nightfall, the Children became agitated.

"What on earth can have happened?"

"Don't worry! I expect they have started chatting to someone. You know what our father is like once he gets started!"

"Yes, but our mother would make sure they got back here in good time. Let's go and see if we can find them."

"Oh, alright, if it will put your mind at rest. Let's go!"

On their way to the farm, they were frightened by the eerie, echoing sounds made by Hyena, a wild and hungry hyena if sounds were anything to go by.

Terrified, the Children started running as fast as they could in the direction of a huge baobab tree. Realising that Hyena had given chase they were desperate to reach the safety of the tree and clamber up into its branches, out of reach of such a wild and hungry creature. Luck was on their side as the animal stumbled at the last moment, giving the Children just the time they needed to reach safety.

Arriving at the baobab tree, Hyena looked up into the branches, shook the horse's tail he had brought with him, put it on the ground and picked up his rattle. As he shook the rattle he fixed his gaze on one of the Children and asked,

"What is your name?"

"My name is Child."

"I'll beat the drum for you to dance, Child."

"Do as you wish. You will not draw me into your magic."

"What is your name?" repeated Hyena.

"My name is Child."

Picking up the horse's tail once again, Hyena began his incantation:

> *I'll beat the drum and Child will dance.*
> *I'll shake the rattle and Child will dance.*

Repeating these lines slowly at first, Hyena gradually increased the speed as he whirled beneath the branches of the baobab tree where the hunter's Children sat watching, doing their utmost to conceal their fear from the wild and hungry Hyena just a few metres beneath them. On and on he went:

I'll beat the drum and Child will dance.
I'll shake the rattle and Child will dance.
And I, Hyena will catch you.

Once again, Child told Hyena that his spell would never work but, undeterred, Hyena repeated the chant seven times, waving the horse's tail, beating the drum and shaking the rattle as he did so. Finally realising that the Children were not to be lured out of the protective baobab tree, Hyena attempted to climb the tree himself but, seeing him coming towards them, the Children jumped down onto the ground, seized Hyena's horse's tail, drum and rattle and started circling the tree, chanting as they went:

"Old man, what is your name?
Old man, what is your name?

Hyena looked down and answered:

Do not ask me, Children.
My Children, do not ask.
Leave the rattle and leave the drum
And find your home again.

Seven times the question was asked:

Old man, what is your name?

And seven times Hyena looked down and answered:

Do not ask me, Children.
My Children, do not ask.
Leave the rattle and leave the drum
And find your home again.

After the seventh time, Child said: "Old man, let me play the drum for you to dance."

As he spoke, he picked up the drum which he began beating, following the rhythm his mind and body had absorbed from his days in his mother's womb. It was not long before Hyena, completely mesmerised, fell out of the huge baobab tree. Falling heavily, he lost consciousness and so the Children made their speedy escape and upon arriving home, they found their parents sitting and chatting. Expecting sympathy as they recounted their eventful evening, it came as a shock to see that their parents had no sympathy whatsoever.

"What do you expect if you go off on your own, especially after dark? Let this be a lesson to you. Never again do we expect to see either of you ignoring our orders".

And so it was that the hunter's Children learned that if they wanted to stay safe, they had to obey their parents. Wisdom and children make poor friends.

Storyteller:	An old lady told me this story on my way here to meet you.
Audience:	Is that so? Then long may your tongue be oiled.
Storyteller:	And long may your ears be greased

Storytelling village: Anyako

Chapter 9

THE TWO HUNTERS

Storyteller: Listen to the story
Audience: So let the story begin
Storyteller: The story falls upon the first Hunter, Ada
Audience: It falls upon the first Hunter, Ada
Storyteller: The story falls upon the second Hunter, Aza
Audience: It falls upon the second Hunter, Aza

Storyteller

Once upon a time in a world we enter only in our dreams, there were Two Hunters, Ada and Aza. Ada, always happy, held firmly to the belief that nothing that happens in this world should be thought of as being so thoroughly evil that it brings nothing but misery; everything must carry somewhere the seeds of goodness even though these may be deeply buried. However Aza, always depressed, saw the world as bringing nothing but evil, pain and suffering. Tired of arguing their very divergent standpoints, they decided to consult their Chief who told each one to go and find a way of proving his personal belief.

So the Two Hunters went their separate ways and one night it so happened that they were both out hunting in the same part of the same forest, and that both of them were wearing headlamps in order to find their way in the dense forest blackness. As they wandered, their attention was unexpectedly drawn to the sound of cracking twigs and snuffling and so each switched off his lamp in order to corner and kill whatever animal was rooting around. All of a sudden the two men collided. Not recognising one another in the blackness of both the night and the forest, they began their conversation as total strangers might do.

"What's your name?" asked Aza.

"My name is 'nothing hurts me'. What's yours?"

"My name is 'everything hurts me'. Did you say your name is 'nothing hurts me'?"

"Yes, I did", confirmed Ada.

"So if I go and find your wife and children and kill them, it won't hurt you?"

"No, it won't," replied Ada very calmly.

So the two men set off for Ada's village where Aza took the Hunter's wife and children and killed them all in front of the happy Hunter who remained silent throughout. Seeing that this atrocity aroused no anger, no tears, no shouts of revenge in Ada, Aza then went to the house where Ada's elderly parents lived, pulled them out of their house and into the compound where he shot them point-blank.

"Doesn't this carnage, this senseless slaughter enrage and hurt you?" he asked.

No," Ada said, unwavering.

Determined to find something which would move his companion to anger or tears of hurt, Aza went back to Ada's house to which he set fire, completely destroying all the contents as well as the house itself.

"Will this destroy you and your crazy ideas?" asked Aza.

"No, it won't," replied Ada, clinging steadfastly to his belief.

"In that case, I know of one last way to test you and see if you will break or not. Follow me!"

So saying, Aza picked up three sharpened sticks and a stone and the Hunters made their way into the heart of the forest. Deeper and deeper they ventured without pausing. Aza looked neither to left nor right, so intent was he on reaching their destination in the fastest possible time. A few hours later, well into the dusky hours of this particular evening, the two men emerged from the forest into a deserted landscape where the only apparent living organism was a vast baobab tree. This same tree, as Aza knew, was the constant eating-place of the three Giant Birds which fed only on human flesh. Using the stone and the three wooden sticks, Aza nailed Ada to the tree and then, putting his face just a few inches from Ada, he shouted,

"This will surely hurt and destroy you along with your lunatic belief.

"No, it will not."

Whether or not Ada was flinching, I really cannot say my friends, as you must remember that his face was obscured from view by Aza's aggressive pose. All we know is that Aza left him there and made his way back through the deep forest, only stopping once he reached home.

The following morning, all the birds, animals and insects which inhabited the silent and deserted night-time world, arrived to see for themselves the Hunter being held prisoner by the huge baobab tree. Knowing that the Giant Birds would not appear until the evening, they wandered off in dribs and drabs to see to their own needs and so Ada endured all alone the fierce heat of the sun and the whipping of the wind as it swept down from the plains of the north.

Towards evening, the rays of the declining sun were eclipsed by the arrival of the three Giant Birds, flying towards the baobab tree and carrying three human carcasses. Some while later, having sated his appetite, the First Bird said,

"In the village of Yor, the Chief has become blind and has been told that there is no hope of a cure. Confined to his palace and unable to carry out his duties, he is more and more morose and his people are more and more dejected."

The Second Bird, now ready to talk, joined the conversation, saying,

"In the village of Adza, the Chief has recently developed a hunchback which has caused some of his counsellors to desert him. The hunch has grown bigger and bigger and now fills the bedroom so that this Chief also is confined to his palace, lonely and sad."

"In the village of Daba, the Chief has lost control of his bladder. Every room in the palace smells of urine so he can no longer go out or receive visitors. He too is lonely and sad," added the Third Bird.

The three Birds fell silent for a while until the First Bird interrupted their private thoughts.

"Nobody but us knows the power of this baobab tree."

"That is true."

"If you take the root, grind it and smear the paste on a hunchback, the swelling will vanish never to return," said the First Bird.

"If you take the bark, boil it and give it to the Chief whose urine flows uncontrollably, he will be cured," added the Second Bird.

"If you take the early morning leaf of the baobab tree and squeeze it onto the eyes of the blind Chief, his sight will be restored," advised the Third Bird.

So caught up were they in their own world that the three Birds completely ignored the man nailed to the tree just a few feet below them and so it was that when morning came, they flew off to track down their new prey. Their departure loosened a leaf which floated down and came to rest on Ada. Its power released the weakened Hunter and so, waiting just long enough to recover some strength, Ada collected the baobab leaves, bark and root and set off for the three villages where he knew he would find the afflicted Chiefs.

He went first to Yor, walked into the palace and told the Chief that he could cure his blindness.

"I need two bags of corn, two drums of corn-oil and two rams."

Once the items were assembled, Ada took the baobab leaves and squeezed the liquid onto the Chief's eyes whose sight was immediately fully restored. Taking the corn, the oil and the rams, Ada went into the fields nearby and prepared a magnificent meal for himself which soon restored him to full health. Summoned to the palace, he was amply rewarded by the happy Chief who bestowed on him the title of Deputy Chief which gave him not only full citizenship of the village but also his own house and servants. Furthermore, The Chief offered him his daughter in marriage and sovereignty over half his extensive kingdom. After a week of living in unaccustomed luxury, Ada asked permission to leave Yor to go on another mission.

This granted, Ada set off for the second village, Adza. Arriving at the Chief's palace, he entered the compound and announced that he could cure the Chief's hunchback. So desperate was the Chief that he was prepared to try anything and he asked Ada what he needed to effect his cure.

"Two bags of corn, two drums of palm-oil and two rams," replied the happy Hunter.

As soon as the items appeared in the compound, Ada took the bark of the baobab tree and ground it into a paste which he smeared all over the Chief's hunch. The cure was instantaneous and those counsellors who had remained loyal to their Chief rose in spontaneous joy and admiration. Some even went so far as to proclaim Ada as a new King. The Chief immediately consulted his Elders and it was decided to enstool him as co-chief with all the associated rights and privileges. After a week, Ada again asked for permission to go on another mission.

When he reached Daba, he found the village almost deserted as the Chief's urine had become a veritable river, polluting the land all around. The Chief remained in his palace with only one faithful servant. When Ada appeared and offered a cure for his affliction, the Chief's first reaction was to refuse as he had lost all hope and was too embarrassed and depressed even to consider that there might be a recipe for success.

It was only because of Ada's persistence that he finally gave in, deciding to give this strange medicine man a chance. After all, his servant reasoned, he had nothing to lose. All that could be lost was already lost.

"What do you need?" asked the Chief.

"Two bags of corn, two drums of corn-oil and two rams."

It took much longer than was usual to find these items as the servant had to go on a long journey, way beyond the polluted kingdom. Nothing living had been seen in the area for a long time. Eventually he returned triumphant and Ada took and chopped the baobab roots before boiling them and offering the liquid to the Chief as a drink.

So revolting was the smell, even to the Chief's urine-soaked senses, that he refused to drink! However his refusal was ignored by the servant who, seizing hold of the Chief's head, tipped it back, pinched his nose and forced his mouth open. The thick, cloudy, brown liquid disappeared down his gullet and within seconds, his bladder began to shrink and the flow of urine dwindled to the merest trickle before stopping completely. The first thing the Chief did was to leave the palace and inspect the flooded landscape. Ada went to the first spot of dry land that he could see and immediately cooked himself another fine meal.

The news spread like wild-fire and the citizens returned to their village to see for themselves the amazing transformation which brought hope for a new and prosperous life in Daba.

On the third day, the Chief invited everyone to a great feast during which he addressed his people,

"I welcome you all back with open arms. I understand and therefore pardon all those who left Daba to seek a living elsewhere. In grateful recognition of the service unstintingly rendered to me throughout all the desperate years of my affliction and also of the part he played in my recovery, I appoint my faithful servant, Dzigbordi, as heir to my kingdom. His successor shall be Ada, the strange medicine man who has cured me and restored not only my life but also the life of this, my ancestral village. Long live Daba!"

80

As in the past, Ada stayed for a week before going to the Chief and seeking permission to leave. Deciding to return to his own native village, the Hunter stopped at a wayside hostelry and ordered a drink. His attention was eventually drawn to a haggard figure who downed one drink after another. Looking closely at him, he eventually recognised the second Hunter, Aza.

"Do you know who I am?" asked Ada.

Ada recounted the full story to Aza who became more and more envious. How could this possibly happen? He remembered thinking that Ada would not live long, nailed to the huge baobab tree in the full glare of the African midday sun.

"Take me to the tree and introduce me as your friend. You have no idea how I have suffered since I left you. I have experienced nothing but pain and destitution. Look at you, happy and well. You can surely be generous to me," pleaded Aza.

"I shall not take you. Your presence would only offend the baobab tree which has been the source of all the good fortune which has recently befallen the Chiefs who endured real suffering for so long."

So the two men went their separate ways and the following day, the miserable Aza called his son, collected a stone and three sticks which he sharpened at one end before setting off for the baobab tree. Arriving late in the afternoon he told his son to nail him to the tree and to leave him there alone. Not long after, the three flesh-eating birds arrived with their human carcasses, perched on the baobab tree and started tearing the flesh which they consumed greedily.

"You remember that Chief who lived in Adza. Well, his hunchback has disappeared and the whole community is flourishing once again. It's a mystery but all I know is that it has happened," said the First Bird.

"You remember the Chief who lived in Daba. He too is fully restored to health and his people are happy and prosperous," added the Second Bird.

"And the Chief of Yor is as healthy as he ever was, able to lead his people once again," concluded the Third Bird.

They fell silent for a while as they digested their meal, but after a while the conversation started up again,

"How did this all happen? Somebody must have been eavesdropping while we were discussing the baobab tree."

"That's very possible. We weren't very careful when we were talking so it's our own fault. We must take care not to do it again."

"I agree. In future we shall be more vigilant. Just think, if we had caught the villain, we would have drunk his blood, eaten his flesh and ground the bones."

As the Third Bird finished speaking, he happened to look down and saw Aza tied only a few feet below.

It was the matter of an instant to swoop down and free him. The First Bird drank his blood, the Second Bird ate his flesh and the Third Bird ground his bones and ate them.

So, my friends, understand that if you go through life expecting evil then all you will find is evil. We can safely assume that Ada went on to enjoy a happy and fulfilling life, visiting in turn the villages where the Chiefs had rewarded him so generously. Never again was he hungry and never again did he have to prove that every misfortune, however calamitous it may seem, holds in it the potential for good, however impossible that might at first appear.

Storyteller:	An old lady told me this story on my way here to meet you.
Audience:	Is that so? Then long may your tongue be oiled.
Storyteller:	And long may your ears be greased.

Storytelling village: Dzelukope

Chapter 10

GOSEVIDE AND DAESINU

Storyteller: Listen to the story
Audience: So let the story begin
Storyteller: The story falls upon Gosevide
Audience: It falls upon Gosevide
Storyteller: The story falls upon Daesinu
Audience: It falls upon Daesinu

Storyteller

Once upon a time, in the settlement of Adza, there lived a hunter called Gosevide and his wife Daesinu. They loved each other very much. They went everywhere together. They did everything together.

"Have you ever seen a couple so much in love?"

"Have you ever known such devotion?"

"Those two are an example to us all."

"I would be happy if my husband showed me even half that much attention.

So ran the comments of all those who knew Gosevide and Daesinu.

Now we are told that every year a special ceremony took place in Adza. The central focus of the ceremony was an ancient ritual in which one woman had to be sacrificed to the gods. How was the woman chosen? Lots were cast amongst all the villagers who, year upon year waited anxiously to learn the name of the chosen one, of she whose life was destined to be offered to the gods.

Imagine then the desperation of Daesinu when her name was drawn. Not only did she have to prepare herself for death, but she also had no husband to support her at the moment of receiving the dreadful news. As you must know, this poor woman could do nothing but weep. So where was Daesinu's husband?

Now you will recall that Gosevide was a hunter and it so happened that he was away in the forest throughout this black day. When he returned late in the evening, Daesinu, whose tears had finally stopped, could not find the words to tell him what was shortly to happen to her. So the hunter and his wife went to bed and it was not until the following morning that Gosevide learned what everyone else in the village knew already; his dear wife was to be taken from him, his Daesinu, his wife and friend with whom he shared everything.

"You shall not die, dearest wife, without me doing all in my power to save you."

"And what if you fail, my husband?"

"Then I shall die with you. My life means nothing to me without you by my side," answered Gosevide heroically.

The following morning, however, this hero, this husband, this man set off hunting once again and during his absence from home the Executioners arrived to take Daesinu away to a secure place where she was closely guarded. Yet again, Daesinu was facing death, all alone. And her husband? Where exactly was he? What exactly could he be doing? We do know that, having failed to kill an animal that day, Gosevide set off for home and that once again he was unaware of what had befallen his wife in his absence.

They say that ignorance is bliss but all we can say for

certain is that our man was seized by a desperate thirst as he journeyed home. Passing through a village, he stopped and asked where he could buy a drink and was told he needed to go to Dogbo, a neighbouring village which had its own special brew. Suddenly happy at the prospect of finding a good drink, Gosevide sang as he walked:

> *Dogo, Dogbo.*
> *Dogbo, Dogbo.*
> *When shall I drink,*
> *Where shall I drink*
> *My sodabi, my sodabi?*
> *I'll drink and drink.*
> *I'll drink and drink.*
> *Then home I'll go,*
> *Then home I'll go*
> *To Daesinu, my Daesinu.*

Arriving at Dogbo, Gosevide was soon enjoying his 'sodabi' but eventually he headed back to Adza, happier and singing louder than ever before. Once home, Gosevide, devoted husband, found his bed and instantly fell fast asleep.

88

Let us now turn our attention to poor Daesinu, passing her final hours under close guard. Only a miserable housefly penetrated her misery and suddenly, glimpsing a ray of hope, Daesinu called to the fly,

"Fly, Fly, come here! I want you to go to my husband Gosevide, and tell him where I am and that I shall be sacrificed in a few hours from now."

"No, I won't do that for you, not after the way you treated me the last time I saw you."

"What do you mean, Fly?"

"See, you don't even remember shooing me away when all I wanted was a little of your porridge."

Having delivered his cruel refusal, the fly left and Daesinu began to weep but gradually her weeping turned to lamenting:

> *Gosevide, Gosevide,*
> *Why is it that you must drink*
> *And lose your sense*
> *Gosevide?*
> *The sheep is sacrificed,*
> *Is sacrificed.*
> *The goat is sacrificed,*

Is sacrificed.
So think of me, your Daesinu,
Your Daesinu
Waiting for the sacrifice,
My sacrifice.

Picking up the strains of the lament, a passing bee decided to go and see who was crying and singing such a mournful song. The moment Daesinu noticed the bee, she began to plead,

"Bee, Bee, come here! I want you to go to my husband Gosevide, and tell him where I am and that I shall be sacrificed in a few hours."

Touched by Daesinu's plight, the bee set off straight away for Gosevide who was sound asleep in bed. The bee flew into first one ear and then the other but, without stirring, Gosevide brushed him away. So the bee buzzed his way into a sleeping nostril and used his sting to wake up Gosevide.

"Come on, rouse yourself, you lazy good-for-nothing husband. Do you not understand that your poor wife is in the forest and about to be sacrificed? How do think she is feeling, all alone as she faces death?

Is this the best you can do for her, sleeping like this?"

Stung into action, Gosevide jumped out of bed, seized his gun and set off for the forest where he soon recognised a distant voice singing a sad and desperate song. As he went further into the trees, the words grew clearer and clearer:

> *Gosevide, Gosevide,*
> *Why is it that you must drink*
> *And lose your sense*
> *Gosevide?*
> *The sheep is sacrificed,*
> *Is sacrificed.*
> *The goat is sacrificed,*
> *Is sacrificed.*
> *So think of me, your Daesinu,*
> *Your Daesinu*
> *Waiting for the sacrifice,*
> *My sacrifice.*

All of a sudden, Gosevide saw both his wife and the Executioners and so he quickly changed course to avoid being noticed. Tree by tree, bush by bush, he drew closer to the scene and found a convenient tree which he climbed so as to have a perfect view of the sacrifice about to unfold before his very eyes.

Gosevide watched while his wife was forced to lie on the forest floor where she was bound from head to toe. Certain that Daesinu could not move at all, the Executioners raised her up high and circled the altar three times, before placing her on the altar itself. With great ceremony, the priest handed the sacrificial dagger to the Chief Executioner. Once, twice, three times, four times, five times, six times the knife was shown to the heavens.

His nerves taut as steel, Gosevide raised his gun, adjusted the sight, found the trigger and fired the bullet only seconds before the ritual knife was to pierce Daesinu's heart. Shot through the chest and clutching the dagger in his right hand, the Chief Executioner staggered forward towards Daesinu and collapsed, slumped right across the terrified woman.

All those who had gathered to watch the sacrifice ran screaming from the scene. They ran this way and that way, that way and this way, they pushed one another, they fell over one another. It was clear to them that the gods had rejected the intended sacrifice and that they

might all become victims of the anger of the gods, just
like the Chief Executioner. Meanwhile, Gosevide was
quick to climb down from the tree and move the body of
the Chief Executioner so as to release his wife from her
captive bonds. Had you been there, you would have
seen Gosevide and Daesinu sobbing together, such was
their relief and joy at being reunited. On the way home,
Daesinu began to question her husband.

"So what did you do when you reached home after

hunting in the forest?"

"I went to bed," was Gosevide's brief reply. Was he perhaps worried about the way this conversation might develop?

"Didn't you notice that I wasn't there?" asked Daesinu.

"It was dark and I was so tired that I just fell into bed without seeing anything at all."

By way of reply, Daesinu began singing to her husband:

> *Your ear is dead, your ear is dead,*
> *You cannot hear, you do not hear.*
> *The day your head, the day your head*
> *Will be cut off, will be cut off,*
> *It's then you'll cry, like me you'll cry*
> *A desperate cry, my desperate cry.*
> *The innocent are killed in war,*
> *The innocent are killed in life,*
> *Pursued to death, like Daesinu.*
> *What chance have they? What chance had I?*

We can now leave Gosevide and Daesinu, who lived the rest of their days in peace and happiness, undisturbed by memories of the Executioners. However, we cannot forget the Executioners as, standing before their Chief, they related the whole story and went so far as to put forward their theory that the gods had killed the Chief Executioner to show their anger at the sacrifice of one of the villagers.

"I do not hold you to account for the tragic death of my Chief Executioner. I shall now withdraw with my most senior Counsellors in order to consider what we have learned and what we must do now," explained the Chief, who rose and left the Executioners still shaking with fear and shock.

Some time later, the Chief returned and spoke again to the assembled Executioners.

"After much careful deliberation, it has been decided by us that our annual ritual must change. We shall no longer sacrifice one of us but instead, we shall select only a sheep or a goat."

And so it was and so it is from that day to this that the villagers welcomed the annual ritual. No longer did fear possess the hearts and minds of the people of Adza. Was there anyone who dared begrudge the loss of a sheep or a goat? And the gods, were they happy?

We must assume they were, as never again did they show such displeasure at any action taken by those they watched over and judged.

Storyteller:	This is the story an old man told me on my way here to meet you.
Audience:	Is that so? The long may your tongue be oiled.
Storyteller:	And long may your ears be greased.

Storytelling village: Klikor

CPSIA information can be obtained
at www.ICGtesting.com
Printed in the USA
LVOW04s1038150516
488339LV00017B/881/P